April 19, 2012

To: West Georgia Library Regional Library

Praise God for "His" "Justice"!

Thank you Carrollton, Georgia for being so Welcoming to our Production Cast & Crew!

Jackie Carpenter

Georgia Justice:

Journey to Faith

By Jackie Carpenter

Georgia Justice
"Journey To Faith"
by Jackie Carpenter

Printed in the United States of America

ISBN 9781612155579

Unless otherwise indicated, Bible quotations are taken from
The King James Version of the Bible.

www.xulonpress.com

Contents

Dedication

I dedicate this book to God. Thank you, Lord, for making me "be still," and during that stillness allowing me to hear what You had to say, and using my fingers to type Your words, which all came together in the end to create this book, *Georgia Justice:"Journey To Faith"*.

Be still and know that I am God

(Psalm 46:8).

Acknowledgments

I would like to acknowledge Pastor Steve Smith, pastor of New Horizons Baptist Church, who in the midst of one of the hardest battles of warfare he has ever been through with his health, encouraged me to write my second book. God bless you, Pastor Steve. Keep your strong faith. And to my wonderful husband, who said to me, "Have you ever thought about writing a second book? I think you should."

Never let me forget to acknowledge my two sons, Jim and Jason, who I am so proud of for so many reasons, but most importantly their dedication to preaching the gospel of Christ. I am so blessed to

have two sons that are both pastors. May God con-

tinue to draw them closer to Himself every day.

Preface

This book is based on actual events. It is based solely on my views and my experiences. It will take you on my journey from believing that I had a lot of faith to the stunning realization that the faith I possessed did not even start to measure up to where it needed to be.

You don't realize that when everything is going along nice and easy in life. You realize that when in the matter of minutes your whole life is turned upside down and your faith is *not* turning you right-side up!

That is where I was: Upside down and seeing no way out! I thought to myself, *How in the world could something like this be happening in my life?* I was in the danger zone!

Submit yourselves therefore to God. Resist the devil and he will flee from you. Draw nigh to God, and he will draw nigh to you (James 4:7-8).

Introduction

Am I dying? I feel as if I am suffocating and choking on my own tears in my own bed. I must be having a nightmare! But how can that be because I am not asleep?

As I tried to sit up I had shortness of breath, my palms were sweating, and my fingers and toes were numb. I did not want to wake up Larry. You see, it was not the first time that had happened. It had been going on for several months and had become normal for me.

I tried to climb out of the bed without making any noise. I was able to get down to the floor and back onto my knees down beside my bed. It was the place I had to get to in order to make the nightmare go away and to be able to breathe normally again. For you see, it is where I knelt before the Lord and prayed for strength. It was strength that I always thought I had, but when tragedy struck all strength was gone.

I was not praying for strength to get me through the tragedy. I was praying for strength to help me crawl from the bed into my prayer closet. If I could just make it that far without dying then I knew once I got there I would be safe from the tormenting thoughts sent by Satan.

I crept from the bedroom and through the darkness until I soon saw the little nightlight that helped guide me along the way into the prayer closet. Once there, all I had the energy to say was, "Here I am again, Lord. Plug me in to life support." And He would gently take me by the hand and guide my eyes to His Word until peace came back, my breathing slowed down, I refocused my thinking, and I was once again able to return to bed.

And he said unto them, I beheld Satan as lightning fall from heaven. Behold, I give unto you power to tread on serpents and scorpions, and over all the power of the enemy: and nothing shall by any means hurt you (Luke 10:18-19).

Chapter One

The Scorpion's Sting

Have you ever entertained the thought of something bad or tragic happening to your family? I try not to think like that. I always try to think positively in most every situation. I love being an optimist and I love being around other positive people. But because I do not typically entertain the thought of something bad happening my mind was totally unequipped and unprepared for what lay in store for my family one summer's eve.

I was in the "danger zone" and I had no clue. How could I have known? Were there any "danger ahead" warnings? How could I have missed it? Was there anything that I could possibly have done to stop this tragedy from taking place? The answer to that question is this: if there was anything that I could have done it was too late. I couldn't change anything afterward. It was too late!

Until that fateful day, life was great and I could not have been happier. I have a great husband, two wonderful sons, and two beautiful daughters-in-law. God had also blessed me with four grandchildren: Hannah, Anna Grace, Patience, and J.J. My parents are the world's best and I had no problems of any kind. Whether it was finances or health, everything was just great! Life could not have been any better than it was at the time. Little did I know that by the end of that very day life would be changed forever for our family. If only I could back up to that moment in time. Oh, how I would have stopped the tragedy!

It was a beautiful June evening and Larry and I had just attended a party for my daughter-in-law Jennifer's dad, Mickey, in Atlanta. He would soon be undergoing a bone marrow transplant so the party was held in his honor. All of his family and friends were there and it was a very touching party. Bittersweet, I guess you could call it. After the party Larry and I drove back to our home in South Georgia. We had driven up in sep-arate vehicles because I went up earlier that day to see the family and Larry had driven up later. Around 9:00 p.m. we said our goodbyes and left the party.

I guess it was about midnight when I finally got back to our home. I was so exhausted that all I could manage to do was take a shower and go to bed. Larry had gotten back an hour earlier so he was already sleeping like a baby. As I jumped out of the shower and hopped into bed I could hardly remember my head hitting the pillow. I was totally clueless as to what was about to happen that was going to impact our family in such a horrific way and change our lives forever. Totally clueless!

Out of nowhere and when I least expected it—while I was sleeping no less—I got stung by the scorpion, Satan. This sting came by way of a terrible tragedy involving my youngest son, Jason. No mother has ever had more love for her sons and so I could have handled it much better if it had happened to me and not my son.

My sting from Satan came on June 28, 2008 by way of one of those dreadful wake-up calls from my dad at 2:00 a.m. telling me that while Jason was guarding his houses the copper thieves returned, there was a struggle, the gun misfired, and one of the alleged culprits had been shot. Billy, Jason's father-in-law, had gone to the site, and in order to get medical attention to the wounded guy, Billy had rushed him to the hospital in his own truck instead of waiting on the ambulance.

My dad told me that he and my mother were going to the hospital and they would keep me informed. I felt sure that this man would get the proper medical care, the police would arrest all three of them, and the nightmare of copper theft would be behind us. Jason had been robbed continuously of copper over the past few weeks and could get absolutely no relief from law enforcement. I started praying while waiting to hear back from my dad and I must have drifted back off into a deep sleep while holding the telephone in my hand.

My second sting from Satan came five hours later when the phone rang again. As I picked it up I was quite sure it was my dad calling to let us know everything was fine, but it was not my dad and that was not the case. It was my daughter-in-law Stephanie (Jason's wife) screaming and crying into the telephone. She was telling me that the man who was wounded had died and my son Jason had been arrested, taken to jail, and falsely accused of felony murder, and her dad may also be arrested. Stunned into awareness, I realized that I was not still sleeping, and this was not a dream. I was awake, and it was Steph on the phone, but I simply could not comprehend what she was saying. It was so farfetched that I just could not wrap my mind around it. How do you deal with something like this?

I immediately tried to call my dad but was told by Mom that he had gone to get Jason's real estate attorney out of bed and let him know what had happened. Jason is a homebuilder and Ron handled the real estate closings each time one of the houses sold, so he and Jason had worked together for years and had formed a genuine friendship as well as a working relationship. This really made it all real to me! It was not a bad dream that I was about to wake up from.

This was a real-life nightmare that I would not wake up from until approximately 10 months later. I managed to call Steph back and let her know that my dad was contacting Ron, and Larry and I were coming up to be with her.

This false accusation led me to a different place in my life—a very dark and scary place. I think it would be fair to say that it was the closest I have ever come to experiencing hell. It was a place of torment, despair, gloom, helplessness, restlessness, and hopelessness.

The sorrows of hell compassed me about

(Psalm 18:5).

For the first time I had been stung by the unthink-able. Never in my life had I ever thought that I would be dealing with something like that. Who would ever think that they would be awakened by a call like that one? It was something I had never even entertained the thought of, and now it was happening in my life and my entire family's life. It not only stung me but every member of our family, including my little 6-year-old grandson who knew something bad had happened but could not understand why his dad had been taken to jail.

I kept thinking to myself, *Dear Lord, why has this happened to my son, his beautiful wife, and their precious little boy? What are we going to do? I have to get up and pull myself together. Oh Lord, I have to wake up Larry and tell him what has happened. I have to do something. I have to get dressed.*

I told Larry that Stephanie had called and said that while Jason was guarding his houses under construction last night there was a bad accident. Larry knew from the call at 2:00 a.m. from my dad that one of the men had been accidentally shot, and I was telling him the sad ending to the ordeal. The young man passed away and Jason had been arrested and charged with murder. Evidently from what Steph said, Jason had called Billy down there also and he may be arrested too. I could not believe the words that were coming out of my mouth. Totally stunned and in a world of disbelief, all I could say was, "This cannot be happening!"

I stressed that Steph did not have any details and that she was totally distraught. I then told Larry about the conversation with my mom, and that Daddy had gone to get Ron. Larry suggested that we get dressed and get up there immediately because they may know more by the time we got there. It was a two-hour drive from our house to Jason and Stephanie's house. My mom and dad were on their way down to Jason and Stephanie's place and J.J. had been taken over to stay with Patty, Steph's mom, and Ron would be meeting us there as soon as he could see Jason and speak with the authorities.

I guess it was somewhere between 9:30 and 10:00 a.m. when we arrived at Jason and Stephanie's. Billy, Steph's dad, had been released and was there along with my parents, Jason's brother Jim, and a couple of their closest friends. Billy looked so worn and weary as he himself had been interrogated all through the night and knew that he may be arrested over what he knew was just a terrible accident. He explained to us everything that had transpired that night and there was no way Jason should have been charged with murder. It sounded like such a tragic accident! We tried to console each other the best we could but everyone was still in shock. Little did we know that everything was about to get much, much worse!

Awake, why sleepest thou, O Lord? Arise, cast us not off for ever. Wherefore hidest thou face, and forgettest our affliction and our oppression? For our soul is bowed down to the dust: our belly cleaveth unto thine earth. Arise for our help, and

redeem us for thy mercies' sake

(Psalm 44:23, 26).

Chapter Two

Rush To Judgment

As each of us sat at Jason's house with swollen eyes and heavy hearts, it was such a relief when Ron came into the living room. But as I saw the look on his face I just knew immediately that I did not want to hear what he had to say! I asked him how Jason was doing and he replied that he was holding up. I asked him when we could go get him and bring him back home and he said not just yet. I asked when I could see him and he said soon he would be able to have three visitors for 15 minutes.

I remember saying, "Ron, what is going on here? You know this was a tragic accident!" He said, "Jackie, I know that and you know that, but when I went to see the judge he said that before I got there the deputy who met with Jason earlier in the day to discuss the copper thefts had already made a plea to the judge requesting that Jason be charged with felony murder. He stated that Jason had been in a rage that afternoon when they met and Jason just wanted to kill someone."

I knew this was a false accusation about Jason, but why in the world would this deputy be saying that? I am Jason's mom and in the 28 years that I have known him and watched him grow from a child into a young man I have never seen Jason in a rage. He was always so calm and in control of his emotions. The statement the deputy had made claiming Jason used curse words included words that I have never in 28 years heard Jason say. Jason had been called to preach six months earlier and he was constantly studying God's Word. Everything the deputy had written about Jason was out of Jason's character.

Jason had been robbed 17 times before he took the extreme measure of guarding the houses himself and he was only doing it because of the advice he had been given by this same deputy. I now know that this false accusation was to defend his own job as he had lost numerous other law enforcement positions. This advice had caused the death of a young man and now the deputy was setting Jason up to take the fall to save his own job! However, this truth did not come to light until 10 months later.

Consequently, the judge was basing his judgment to charge Jason with felony murder on this deputy's statement and written report. The judge did tell Ron that he had never met this deputy before and that he must be new on the force, but that did not change the outcome. Jason was being charged with felony murder based on false accusation by this deputy. As we sat together in a family circle around the living room we all had a sick feeling in our stomachs.

All that any of us could do was look to each other for comfort but it was still not enough to bring Jason back home to his family. I felt totally help-less as Jason's mother. All that I wanted to do was see Jason and know that he was okay. I could not take a full breath until I could see Jason for myself. Unbeknownst to us at this time, within the next 24 hours this same deputy would have the other two alleged culprits back down at the crime scene along with a civil suit attorney and Fox 5 News saying that Jason was in a rage and had executed their cousin. That was their side of the story and that is what made the headlines, along with Jason's picture betraying him as a murderer. It appeared that a whole lot of plotting and planning had been going on with these three men over the past 24 hours as my son sat in a jail cell and our family sat in shock.

Two more false statements had emerged and we were still trying to wrap our minds around the first false statement that made absolutely no sense. Why had there been such a "rush to judgment" and why were the news media trying my son's case and convicting him of murder through all of the blogs they continued to post based on everything but the truth?

Why were the news media having a field day with these false accusations? They knew they only had one side of the story, so why did they continue to portray that side as the truth?

We could say nothing to counteract these statements. For 10 months we would be under a "gag order" not able to say anything, not one word, not even to our friends. Nothing made sense anymore except for one thing: I knew in my heart that this deputy had gotten with these two other men and started a conspiracy against Jason. But why? Why were they meeting with a civil suit attorney so soon? Why aren't they grieving over their cousin?

False witnesses did rise up; they laid to my charge

things that I knew not (Psalms 35:11).

Chapter Three

Dangerous Flirtations

T he next morning as I awoke, the emotions hit me like a ton of bricks. I thought to myself: *Oh God, this cannot be happening! I do not have what it takes to face this day! My head hurts, my heart hurts, my eyes hurt, my son is in jail (and should not be), and my cousin Debbie called to say Jason is on the front page of the newspaper, so why don't I just go back to bed, go to sleep, and never wake up!* Those were the thoughts I was dealing with in the aftermath. I was still not able to see straight through all of the fallout. I could not think with a clear mind as my thought patterns were going in several different directions all at the same time.

Satan was dictating my every move. He kept me in a state of confusion and depression. But there was one small problem with Satan's plan. There were some things that I had to do. I had to go to work and I had to feed my dogs. I had to take care of Larry, as he was hurting also. I had to continue to check on my parents, my son Jim and his family, and most importantly, I had to take care of Steph and J.J.

Also, Jason had business matters that he needed my help with and I had to try to keep Steph from totally falling apart. J.J. didn't understand why his daddy was still in jail and we could not give him a straight answer as to when his daddy would be coming home. Satan was draining every ounce of strength out of me daily, but the world was continuing to revolve and nothing was stopping for our broken hearts and confused minds. Isn't it remarkable that the times in life when we need to think the clearest are the times when we are the most confused?

The newspapers and the bloggers would not give us a break. Jason's picture was constantly smeared across the front page portraying him as a murderer. False witnesses were coming forth. False accusations were being given to the news media. And we couldn't stop it! We were not even allowed so much as to speak with a reporter.

"Jason is being abused in jail," Satan would whisper. "He is going to die in there and there is nothing you can do to stop it!" Satan is a dark creature that attacks our minds when we are most vulnerable and our defenses are down. As I said, I was asleep when I got stung, and it's the scariest place that I have ever been in my life.

Why is this happening? This can't be happening! I refuse to believe any of this. I am going back to bed. I don't want to see anybody. I don't want to talk to anybody. I just want the world to leave me alone. Nobody understands! I would feel as the tears started to flow. And Satan would say, "That is right, Jackie, nobody can help you!"

My husband would tell me that the pastor wanted to speak with me on the telephone and I would say I could not talk with him. Satan would say, "That's right, Jackie, you don't need to talk with him because he can't help you." My husband would say that my

Sunday school teacher was on the telephone and I would say I couldn't talk to her. So Satan would say, "That's good, Jackie, she cannot help you. There is no help. Go back to bed and go to sleep. You are in a hopeless situation." It seemed like every time the telephone rang it was just more bad news. Just to hear it ring set my nerves on edge. There was never anything good—it was all doom and gloom.

Larry would say, "Jackie, you have got to get a hold of yourself. You are making yourself sick." Then Satan would say, "See, even Larry doesn't understand how you feel. He thinks that you are being selfish, that you are only thinking about yourself, but you should not be thinking about anybody but yourself. Nobody understands how your heart hurts, and why you cannot stop crying, and why you are so weak and tired. Just go back to bed and stay there." Even when

I tried to pray it was almost as if I couldn't. I couldn't

think straight. I couldn't concentrate on any one thing

long enough to finish any given task, whether it was

praying or working.

I was just going through the motions of life and I

knew that Satan had come between God and me. I

don't know when it happened or how it happened.

I thought I had faith strong enough to endure any-

thing. But I guess prior to this tragedy my faith had

not had much to endure. Both of my sons had been

in car wrecks but those were different because you

knew the outcome immediately and thanked God for

His protection of their lives. No one knew what the

outcome in this situation would be. This ordeal was

a true test of my faith and it would last for 10 long

months. For that period everyday was like walking "through the valley of the shadow of death."

I kept thinking, *Oh God, where are You? Why can't I feel Your presence? Why are You letting this happen? I love You Lord. I am Your child. I have served You my whole life. How did Satan gain control of my mind and body? How did I allow this to happen? I cannot control the darkness. I cannot control the depressing thoughts that I am having. I can't do anything without crying. Oh dear Lord in heaven, I really do not know how much more of this I can take. Will there ever be joy in our family again? Please help us!*

As Larry and I drove to visit Jason and check on the rest of the family I cried all the way for two solid hours. I thought there were no more tears but there just seemed to be a bottomless well. The only thing there was never a lack of was crying. Once we got there I tried to remain strong. There was so much to do and everyone needed encouragement. What I gave them was false encouragement, as I just tried to help them make it through one more day. However, inside I knew that it was not real.

On the drive back home my heart started to fall apart again. The wails would start coming from deep down somewhere inside my broken heart, and for the two-hour drive home there was nothing heard in our car but crying. I brought my knees up to my chest, formed my body into a little ball, and cried myself to sleep. How sad this had to be for Larry as he drove for two solid hours just listening and being patient with me. When we finally made it back to South Georgia all that I had the strength left to do was go to bed and cry myself to sleep and hope that I never had to wake up and face another day like that one. Oh Lord, how I missed Jason. I missed calling him and hearing him talk and make me laugh. I missed hearing him tell me his plans for the day or asking me to type something up for him.

I prayed, "Lord, please take care of my son in that hellhole that Satan has drawn him into. You are the only one that can take care of him in there. He is in there with the worst of the worst and I am so helpless to him. What do you want me to do? I feel like I am so far away from You right now. And I feel like Satan is stalking me. Why can't I focus? My mind is running a relay race in the wrong direction and I cannot slow it down. I don't know what is going to happen to all of us, but I do know that this family is a family of born-again Christians and together we will make it

through. But in the meantime, the only thing that I am

able to do is to cry."

They that sow in tears shall reap in joy

(Psalm 126:5).

Wherefore seeing we also are compassed about

with so great a cloud of witnesses, let us lay aside

every weight, and the sin which doth so easily

beset us, and let us run with patience the race that

is set before us. Looking unto Jesus the author

and finisher of our faith; who for the joy that was

set before him endured their cross, despising the

shame, and is set down at the right hand of the

throne of God. For consider him that endured

such contradiction of sinners against himself,

lest ye be wearied and faint in your minds

(Hebrew 12:1-3).

That is exactly the way I physically felt: like my body had grown so weary and weighted down with sorrow that my mind was on the verge of fainting. I prayed, "Oh Jesus, I am so sorry. I know what this family is going through right now is so mild in comparison to what You endured for each one of us. Now I feel so guilty that I bothered You with all of this. How disappointed You have to be in me." Then in a small, sweet voice I could hear my dear Lord say, "Hold on my child. Joy comes in the morning. Weeping only lasts for the night!"

Chapter Four

In the Midst of Confusion

Hear me speedily O Lord, my spirit faileth, hide not

thy face from me, lest I be like unto them that go

down into the pit (Psalm 143:7).

I cannot get past the vision of tears rolling down Jason's face as I looked at him for the first time through the prison glass. For the rest of my life that is one memory that I will never be able to erase: my son wearing a prison uniform with red and white stripes (symbolizing murderer). I could not touch him, hold him, or tell him it would be okay. What if prison was to become Jason's home? It was so much more than I could handle!

During the 15-minute visit with Jason he requested that Larry and I go back down to the construction site and return his truck to his house. It was another gut-wrenching moment as we drove down to the construction site to get the truck. As we got out and walked up to it I saw his work cap on the dashboard. How many times had I seen my son wear that cap? It was worn out, just like his mind and body at that point in time.

When Larry cranked up the truck it became apparent that Jason had been listening to a gospel CD that was still playing as he had turned off his truck. Tears welled in my eyes as I looked down and saw many other gospel CD's lying on his console.

What a testimony to know that my son had been listening to God's Word as he got out of his truck that fateful night.

Nine days following the bond hearing Steph and I were requested to meet the lead investigator on the case at their house. The agent helped us go through files in order to find Jason's passport since it had to be confiscated before Jason could be released on bond. When we entered Jason's office I saw a picture sitting on his desk of J.J. praying. On his office walls he had posted Sunday school notes and Scriptures to study before he taught his next Sunday school lesson. That sight spoke volumes to me of my son's faith in Jesus Christ. I knew that God was with Jason through the whole ordeal.

Everything I saw edified Christ. There was nothing for Jason to be ashamed of when what he owned would be rummaged through by authorities. What a testimony it was to the lead investigator who was looking at Jason's things in absolute amazement. I know in my heart that he had to be thinking, *Something here just doesn't add up to what I have been told.*

A picture paints a thousand words and whether someone was going through Jason's truck or his home, everything they saw showed what a true man of God Jason was. I now believe this was the first thing that led me back into my close relationship with God. Seeing how close Jason was to God steered me through the fog when I could not see. I was seeing a glimpse of God again because of my son's testimony. At that moment standing in Jason's office and seeing

God everywhere I turned, I may have been seeing God through Jason's eyes but at least I was seeing God instead of Satan.

The only place that I could cope with this at all was in my prayer closet. It seemed as though it was every night that I tried to climb out of the bed without making any noise, get down to the floor, and back onto my knees beside my bed. That was the place I had to get in order to make the nightmare go away and to be able to breathe normally again. For that is where I knelt before the Lord and prayed for strength. It was strength that I always thought I had but when tragedy struck all strength was gone. Satan had depleted me of all my strength and he was trying desperately to take away my life. If he took away my son, he would take away my life as well. That was Satan's mission and I could feel it in my soul!

I was not praying for strength to get me through the tragedy. I was praying for strength to help me crawl from the bed into my prayer closet. If I could just make it that far then I knew I would be safe from Satan's tormenting thoughts because my prayer closet was my refuge from Satan. It was the one and only area of my life where Satan could not get to me. I had to fight him every step of the way because he did not want me to get there. He did not want me to get too close to God. Satan wanted me to doubt God and feel as though I did not have any energy to try to make it there. Satan told me to go back to bed, but I did not listen to him. I could not listen to him, for if I went back to bed I would surely die. My only strength was God's strength for without God I would not sur-

vive the nightmare.

Chapter Five

Warning: Danger Ahead

O ur whole world had fallen apart in a matter of minutes. The question became "what do I do now?" The way that I saw it was I had two choices. I could listen to Satan and slowly give up my life, be of no help to anyone, and become another heartache the family would have to deal with. Or, I could put all of my trust in God and try to hold onto that peace I obtained in the prayer closet. That is what I wanted more than anything else in the whole world. I wanted that peace and that miracle that God promised He would give me in the book of Psalms.

I wanted to hide under the shadow of the wings of the Almighty God day and night. However, God tells us not just to *hide* there but to *abide* (live under) His wings for protection. God didn't want me running to Him just when I was in crisis mode. God wanted me to live and commune with Him daily. Under His wings I was totally safe and secure. God would take care of everything. He told me so in His Word.

He that dwelleth in the secret place of the most High

shall abide under the shadow of the Almighty

(Psalm 91:1).

Psalm 91 says that God sent angels to watch over me, Jason, and the rest of the family. That means that God had angels keeping watch over Jason in Cell Block A. Isn't God the only One who can keep us totally protected anyway? If it were not for those angels He has put in place to guard our steps each and every day how would any of us come to the end of the day without harm besetting us? God protected me from the adversary and Psalms reminded me that He would deliver me from the nightmare.

There was only one problem. I could not stay in my prayer closet. I had to come out and face the real world. That is where I was most vulnerable. It seemed that everywhere I went I heard something from someone that raised doubt in my mind about Jason's future. Even those whom I am sure meant well would say something that would raise my doubt. That was Satan's goal. Satan knew as long as he could insert a shade of doubt into my mind, I was not totally depending on God and God's promises. The attorneys had made a point of telling us more than once that nobody was our friend, we could talk to no one about the case, and if we did it would only hurt Jason.

I remained in constant contact with my prayer partner, Cynthia. Many times I would call her up and could not even utter a word, and she would just start praying. She prayed me through so many days. I didn't have to explain anything to her, she just knew. She knew the hurt. She knew that I was dealing daily with Satan and his minions. When Cynthia prayed with me Satan fled. She also attended a ladies prayer meeting one day a week and that is where Cynthia would fire up the prayer chain.

She called the 700 Club throughout the process and the 700 Club had prayer partners that would pray also. The prayer chain reached from Georgia to New York. Thousands of people were praying for my son. There is so much power in prayer. Then came the daily dreaded end of the day. I really feared seeing the sun go down. I always made it a point to have my Bible study right before going to bed and as I would drift off to sleep I would be in the process of praying as sleep took over my weary and exhausted body.

I really did try to keep my guard raised against Satan. I know that in my prayer closet I never doubted God. However, I could not sleep in my prayer closet even though I came close more than once. Even though I would pray myself to sleep, once in that state of sleep all of my defenses were low. I fought through the day but I was too tired to fight through the night. I was so sleep deprived that even through the day I was in a zombie-like state. I just went through the motions of life.

It was in the darkest hour of the night, when we were asleep and most vulnerable, that the intruder invaded my mind with bad dreams and nightmares, my breathing became erratic and I began hyperventilating, and I awakened to thoughts of terror!

God tells us in Psalm 91 that we shall not be afraid of the terror by night and when I abruptly sat up in bed trying to breathe I knew that if I could get to the prayer closet I would live through the nightmare. I read it in God's Word and it was planted in my mind.

There was a war going on between God and Satan and my sanity was at stake. Jason's entire future was at stake. The lives of my family members were at stake. Everything we had in this life at that moment in time was at stake. How could everything you have in life be brought to ruins in a matter of minutes? After a lifetime of building dreams and families, how could everything be brought to ruins in such a short span of time?

Thou shall not be afraid of the terror by night

(Psalm 91:5).

If I did not have my Bible study and I did not know what God had said then I would have had limited defense against Satan. The torment was so much bigger than me. I awoke to it every morning and I went to bed with it every night, awaiting Satan's vicious attack that I knew would come the minute that I yielded to sleep.

PSALM 91.

A Miracle

HE that dwelleth in the secret place of the most High shall abide under the shadow of the Almighty. 27:5; 32:7; Is. 32:2

2 I will say of the LORD, He is my refuge and my fortress: my God; in him will I trust. 142:5

3 Surely he shall deliver thee from the snare of the fowler, and from the noisome pestilence. 124:7

4 He shall cover thee with his feathers, and under his wings shalt thou trust: his truth shall be thy shield and buckler. 17:8

5 Thou shalt not be afraid for the terror by night; nor for the arrow that flieth by day; [Is. 43:2]

6 Nor for the pestilence that walketh in darkness; nor for the destruction that wasteth at noonday. *lays waste*

7 A thousand shall fall at thy side, and ten thousand at thy right hand; but it shall not come nigh thee.

8 Only with thine eyes shalt thou behold and see the reward of the wicked. 37:34; Mal. 1:5

9 Because thou hast made the LORD, which is my refuge, even the most High, thy habitation;

10 There shall no evil befall thee, neither shall any plague come nigh thy dwelling. [Prov. 12:21]

11 For he shall give his angels charge over thee, to keep thee in all thy ways. Matt. 4:6; Luke 4:10.

12 They shall bear thee up in their hands, lest thou dash thy foot against a stone. Matt. 4:6

13 Thou shalt tread upon the lion and adder: the young lion and the dragon shalt thou trample under feet. *cobra · serpent*

14 Because he hath set his love upon me, therefore will I deliver him: I will set him on high, because he hath known my name.

15 He shall call upon me, and I will answer him: I will be with him in trouble; I will deliver him, and honour him. 50:15; Is. 49:8

16 With long life will I satisfy him, and shew him my salvation.

Chapter Six

The Serpent's Lies

Surely the serpent will bite without enchantment

(Ecclesiastes 10:11).

W aking up to the smell of coffee brewing instead of the anxiety of sweaty palms was such a relief. At least I knew that I had made it through one more night. More than anything I just wanted to start the day out with positive thoughts. As I walked into the kitchen I asked Larry if maybe we could just take the day off, go to the mall, have lunch, and just spend some good quality time away for a little while. He agreed that we needed a break and so far it had been a very peaceful morning.

As we drove to the mall we stopped along the way for breakfast. As we were having breakfast and talking I started to get an uneasy feeling, like something was just not right at home. I tried to ignore it, but as we arrived at the mall I had this feeling deep down inside that something was wrong. It was the day of Jason's arraignment. No one could attend but Jason and his attorneys. It was supposedly just a simple process, a routine procedure more than anything else. It just seemed like anytime Jason underwent a legal proceeding it never turned out positively. Nothing ever seemed to go in our favor. We were told that there was nothing for Larry and I to worry about, but I just had this gut feeling that something was wrong. Satan started filling my head with bad thoughts but I tried to get them out of my mind and continue having a nice day with my husband.

As I went in and out of the stores I could not help but notice all of the people that were there. I was watching the people more than anything else. I wondered how many of them were facing a major battle in their lives? Was I the only one? Were all of the people around me carefree, with nothing weighing them down, nothing that had kept them awake last night, and no problems to worry about? That is how I was a few months ago. I could go outside my house without a worry or care in the world. Yet life was not that way anymore.

Everything changed on June 28, 2008 within a matter of minutes. I didn't go anywhere without worrying. Would it ever be the same again? Would our family ever experience peace again? I just wanted to scream out, "Do any of you feel like I do? Am I the only one here whose heart hurts so bad that I can hardly walk around this mall and breathe at the same time?"

Satan would never even let me entertain the thought of our family enjoying peace again. He would immediately put visions in my mind of Jason in prison, with Steph and J.J. all alone. It seemed life would never be the same again. I had made the comment to Larry that if anything happened to Jason I did not think that I would live through it and Larry had mentioned my statement to Jim, my oldest son. I guess what I meant to say was, if Jason had to go to prison I do not think that my flesh would be able to fight Satan anymore. My defenses would be so low that I would not be able to keep him from totally destroying my body.

Jim, Jen, and my three granddaughters are so precious. Jim is a pastor and they are such a sweet church family, but I could see the worry in Jim's eyes when he said that no matter what the outcome with Jason that Hanni, Anna Grace, and Patience still needed their Gommi. My grandbabies had always called me Gommi, short for grandmommy.

There was so much tension in our family. No one had any peace. We all knew that Jason had been wrongfully accused of a crime, but it had to run its course until the truth came out, one way or the other.

There were no shortcuts to get to the end result so that life could resume with some sense of normalcy. Attorneys were right there to remind me that our life very well may never be normal again. There was never any encouragement from anyone at anytime outside of my prayer closet. How long would it take to run its course? Would our family have the endurance to finish the race or would we lose someone we love to grief before we crossed the finish line?

I went into the restroom and put some cold water to my face and tried once again to think about something positive. Just as I started feeling better and had gained my composure my cell phone rang. It was Jason telling me that at the arraignment he was not only charged with felony murder, but also four other charges on top of that, including three counts of aggravated assault and one count of illegal posses-

sion of a firearm, for a total of five charges laid to his

account instead of one, and the trial date had been

set for April 13, 2009. I could not utter a word...I was

totally speechless!

My soul longeth yea even fainteth for the courts of

the Lord, my heart and my flesh crieth out for the

Living God (Psalm 84:2).

No wonder I had felt as though I was undergoing

a nervous breakdown earlier, for it was at the very

same time that Jason was in front of a judge being

charged with five charges instead of one and another

date had been placed over his head. I guess I must

have been there with him in spirit because what I felt

at the mall was the exact same thing I would have felt had I been sitting in the courtroom! It was the same type of ending to the day as there had been over the past few months. It only continued to get worse as the days went by. I thought to myself, *Oh God, where are You? Please let me feel Your presence. Dear Lord, I don't know how much more of this my physical body can endure.*

Hear my voice, O God, in my prayer: preserve my life from fear of the enemy (Psalm 64:1).

On the drive home Larry and I both were very quiet, as if we were both in a trance. So much for our day away from everything. There was no such thing as getting away from the nightmare. It followed us everywhere. It consumed our every thought day and night. We were both just trying to rationalize what had happened at the arraignment.

As I looked out of the car window I could see that it was getting dark. What a long day it had been. I tried to enjoy the time with Larry as much as I could, but it was like my mind was divided between good thoughts and bad thoughts. Unfortunately the bad thoughts outweighed the good and that kept me in a continuously confused state of mind.

As I prepared for bed I told Larry that I had not prepared myself for what had happened at the arraignment. For some reason I continued to believe that somewhere down the line things would turn around, the truth would emerge, and things would start getting better. Larry said, "That time has not yet come."

I thought to myself, *Will it ever come?*

As I turned off the lights and began praying, my mind was starting to entertain scary thoughts. I did not want to discuss them with Larry, or anyone else for that matter, because if I discussed them with any of the other family members that would just invite them to share the same thoughts I was having, and the thoughts were lies from the deceiver! Jesus was the only One whom I could share them with and so I prayed myself to sleep.

When I remember thee upon my bed, and meditate on thee in the night watches. Because thou hast been my help, therefore in the shadow of thy wings will I rejoice **(Psalm 63:6-7).**

Times-Herald
Established 1865
Newnan, Georgia
ISSN NO. 0883-2536
50 cent

Chapter Seven

No Lifeguard on Duty

Have you ever given any thought as to how much we depend on God to get us through each and every day? Wouldn't we be in trouble if God hung a sign down from heaven that said, "NO LIFEGUARD ON DUTY...LIVE LIFE AT YOUR OWN RISK"! How scary would that be, to go through a storm of life, with no hope of being rescued?

I remember that when my boys were little I was always such an overprotective mother because they were both so precious to me. I kept my eyes on them continuously because I could not stand the thought of anything bad ever happening to either one of them. However, when they grew up and moved out on their own I could not protect them anymore. Instead, they were protecting their own families.

When this terrible accident happened I started blaming myself. I knew that Jason had been a victim of copper theft in the homes he was constructing. I knew that he could not get any relief from law enforcement. I knew that he was planning to guard the houses that night because a deputy had met him earlier in the day and advised him to do it.

So why did I not go down there with him? I knew it was not a good idea for him to do it, but I under-stood what he was planning to do. The deputy had told him earlier that day law enforcement would be patrolling nearby and how he could make a citizen's arrest should the need arise. It sounded very simple.

I thought that since Jason had already been robbed three times that week no one would rob him yet again. Jason was sitting in the woods guarding the houses just in case and I thought it was terrible that he was in that position. But if he was going to get any relief from the robberies what other choices were there? Regardless, why didn't I go and sit with him in the woods?

Those homes were his livelihood and each robbery was costing him approximately $6,000. Come Monday he was going to hire a security guard. It would all get much better then. I just thought if law enforcement officers were patrolling the area they would be of more help to him than me. All he had to do was call and they would be right there, so Jason was told.

It was terrible dealing with all the thefts, but we were dealing with something much worse afterward. The unexpected did happen and when the white van drove up at 12:45 a.m. Jason's nightmare started unfolding. He called 911 and then he called his father-in-law because he was scared to death and he had no idea how many were in the van. Law enforcement was nowhere near the area and once Jason called 911 the officers got lost.

The deputy had advised Jason earlier that day that law enforcement would be made aware that Jason was on his own guarding the houses and assured Jason they would be patrolling the area. They knew what Jason was doing and because the officers got lost his father-in-law Billy arrived first. The fact of the matter is, law enforcement officers were not aware of what Jason was doing and they were on the other side of town getting gas when they received the 911 call and didn't have a clue how to get to where Jason was. Once again the deputy had let Jason down!

When Billy drove up behind the white van, got out of his truck, and approached the van unarmed, Jason had no choice but to come out of hiding to protect Billy. They ordered the three men out of the van, advising them they were not going to hurt them and that law enforcement was on the way. But because of the rebellion of one of the men the gun was accidentally fired and hit that man. Everything that could go wrong went wrong and my son was charged with felony murder and four additional charges.

Note: The case in its entirety is found in my book *The Bridge: Between Cell Block A and a Miracle Is Psalm 91*. It goes into great detail regarding all of the events that transpired on the night of June 28, 2008 and the trial that took place on April 13-16, 2009.

On the night of June 28, 2008 I knew Jason was guarding his houses and I prayed for my son. I had total peace that Jesus was there with him, for Jesus was his "Lifeguard." Yet Satan was telling me there was "No Lifeguard on Duty." He was attempting to twist my mind into thinking Jesus had deserted my son that fatal night.

Trust in the Lord with all thine heart and lean not unto thy own understanding. In all thy ways acknowledge Him and He will direct thy paths (Proverbs 3:5-6).

I had to keep my guard up. I knew that God was Jason's Lifeguard that night and He is always on duty protecting His children. At the same time, I was reminded of what I had read in God's Word so many times: "God's ways are not our ways."

God reminded me that I had called Jason on the site at 10:12 p.m. and he went over everything with me that the deputy had advised him to do. After I hung up I prayed for Jason and God had given me the assurance that Jason was not alone because He was there also! Our family simply had to stand strong in God's Word.

God is our refuge and strength, a very present help in time of trouble (Psalm 46:1).

Chapter Eight

911 or 91:1
(What Is Your Emergency?)

I t was cold in the courtroom. The room was packed but there were many people I did not know. News media and television cameras seemed to be everywhere. The judge was saying something but I could

not bring myself to focus on what he was saying.

I could not believe what was actually happening. I

never thought we would be sitting there and enduring

a murder trial. I always thought the truth would set us

free before we had to bear such a cross of humilia-

tion and shame.

I wanted so desperately to cry and I couldn't.

Where were my tears? I was too scared to cry. I just

wanted to scream and run but I was too scared. It

seemed to be all that I could do to breathe. Larry was

squeezing my hand to the point that it was hurting.

Jason was just standing there looking totally help-

less once again. My family all looked so sad and then

suddenly all that I could hear was the gavel come

down and the judge saying that Jason would be

spending the next 30 years in some federal peniten-

tiary. I could hear people screaming and there was

total chaos. I saw them coming over to Jason and

putting the handcuffs back on him.

Stephanie had run down and grabbed Jason so

they could not put the handcuffs back on him and

another deputy was pulling her away from him. I could

hear her crying and screaming for them not to take

Jason away from her. My parents were crying while

other friends and family were hugging and trying to

comfort them. I looked back down front and Jason

was now gone. I heard someone crying, but I could

not tell where it was coming from. It sounded like a

child. I looked down and it was J.J. standing to my

right side. He was crying and begging me not to let

them take his daddy away.

I took J.J. home with me but I could not get him to stop crying. I could not breathe and I could not believe what was happening. I got J.J. to lie down on the bed with me and to rest but he kept crying that he wanted his daddy.

My God, my God, why hast thou forsaken me? Why art thou so far from helping me, and from the words of my roaring? O my God, I cry in the daytime, but thou hearest not; and in the night season, and am not silent (Psalm 22:1-2).

I could not breathe so I called 911. I tried to reach the telephone on the nightstand and was able to dial 911. I could hear the operator saying, "What is your emergency?" I tried to speak to her but I could

only say, "He won't stop crying and I can't breathe."
I could hear the operator saying, "Ma'am what is the
problem?" I could no longer speak into the phone.
There was no time for paramedics. I would never live
until they arrived. I dropped the phone and tried to get
to my Bible on the nightstand. I had to get to Psalm
91, my life support. I did not need 911 as much as I
needed Psalm 91:1.

I could not get to it, and at about that time I opened
my eyes. It was not J.J. that had been crying but my
dog Bojangles. He was hungry. I was shaking all over
and trying to get to my Bible. I could see that it was
light outside. The telephone rang and I answered it. It
was Larry telling me that he had been trying to call to
wake me up, as it was almost 11:00 a.m. I had been
dreaming!

I don't understand this, I thought to myself. I was having a nightmare in the daytime. That was something new. Was there such a thing as a "daymare"? The bad dreams usually came in the pitch black of night. *Oh God, what was Satan doing to my mind?*

I remembered God and was troubled: I complained, and my spirit was overwhelmed. Thou holdest mine eyes waking: I am so troubled that I cannot speak (Psalm 77:1).

I turned in my Bible to Psalm 91 and the Lord gave me the following verse: *Thou shall not be afraid of the terror by night;* nor *the arrow that flieth by* day (Psalm 91:5).

I had to make myself get up, as hard as it was. It was Friday and I had to drive to the Newnan house and cook dinner for the family. We continued to get together on Friday night the same way we always had. We tried to keep things as normal as possible for the kids' sake. I had no idea how I was going to do all that I had to do with this horrible "daymare" still weighing so heavily on my mind.

On that particular day Satan started out trying to destroy me and continued his plan during my two-hour drive to Newnan. It was such a beautiful day and it had not yet had the chance to reach 90 degrees. I was just trying to enjoy the drive as I passed through 10 small towns on my drive to Newnan and for the first time in 15 years I started noticing that each of the towns had either a jail or a courthouse. Why had I never paid any attention to them before? At each one

Satan would point it out. I usually never even noticed

them, but it seemed that was all that I noticed that

day. Isn't it amazing how our thought processes can

completely change when we are in a crisis? I could

not escape the torment!

I had just finished preparing dinner and the family

had started arriving. When Jason, Steph, and J.J.

arrived I just ran and grabbed Jason and started hug-

ging him. He asked me what was wrong and I said

it was nothing, that I had just been missing him that

day and that it was good to see him. Thank God that

what I had that morning was a horrible dream and

Jason was still with us at least for that day. Was God

preparing my heart and mind for what I was going

to be dealing with somewhere in the not too distant

future? *There is not one person in our family that will be able to handle it if that is the final outcome,* I thought to myself.

Satan had been busy with me that morning and that night he was working overtime with my family. He was controlling their conversations. There was so much worry, so much doubt, so much hurt, and so much pain. It was all bad and nothing good. Deep down I knew that each one of them there in the house had been undergoing the same tormenting thoughts from Satan that I had been dealing with.

The confused state of mind that we were living in was not from God, for God is not the "author of confusion." The cloud of doubt that Satan had sent over each one of our minds was not from God. Satan never gave us the chance to entertain the thought that God would bring His child through this storm of life! Satan left our minds in the daylight hours drowning in the deep sea of hopelessness and in the night watches we were drowning in our own tears.

I always felt like crying, but I couldn't around my family. I had to stay strong for them. Satan wanted me weak, for he was out to kill me. Satan was also tormenting my family and I don't think any of them were sleeping any better at night than I was. Satan was on a rampage to devour our entire family, but I wasn't about to allow him. For it was the love for my precious family that God had blessed me with that kept me fighting Satan. If it wasn't for that strong bond of love along with the assurance that my God lives within me, I would have given up the morning after the "daymare."

Put on the whole armour of God, that ye may be able to stand against the wiles of the devil. For we wrestle not against flesh and blood, but against principalities, against powers, against the rulers of the darkness of this world, against spiritual wickedness in high places

(Ephesians 6:11-12).

Chapter Nine

Fragile and Broken: Handle With Prayer

How many mornings do we get out of bed, go through our normal routines of everyday life, and not give God thanks for letting us get through another night without tragedy striking our families? How often do we just take each day for granted? In looking back about six months before I was one of those people. I always thanked God for another day and I always prayed in the morning for God to protect our family that day. How much of that praying was just routine praying, saying the same thing day after day out of repetition?

I now look at life through different eyes—eyes that had cried so many tears and washed away so much dirt from everyday life that I now had a clear view of my own life and the way that I had been living life. I did not like what I was seeing: I never observed what others around me were going through. For example, noticing those jails and courthouses in all of those towns that I had been going through for 15 years for the very first time. How many times had I prayed for the families inside those places? How many times had I ever given that even one moment of thought? It wasn't until my loved one was placed inside of a jail cell and courtroom. I stopped and noticed because it involved my family and not some stranger's family.

I kept asking myself why God did not prevent the tragedy. However, I know that the Bible says God's ways are not our ways and God's thoughts are not our thoughts, and one of my favorite verses says, "all things work together for good for those that love the Lord." I know that God had a plan and I only saw a small part of it, but instead of fully trusting God to deliver Jason from the nightmare I started turning every ounce of my energy into trying to do it myself.

I became a private investigator, a sheriff's deputy, a defense attorney, a prosecutor, and a judge. I studied days and nights trying to solve the entire misrepresented situation. My immune system was very low because I was not taking care of myself. I wasn't sleeping and I only fell asleep when I was exhausted from doing research. I wore myself completely out.

I started my research first thing in the morning and I didn't stop until night. Then I would have my Bible study and go to bed.

I had gotten so weak and tired that I had to go to the doctor for a checkup, at which time I was told that I was in need of a blood transfusion. My body had become very fragile. That is just the way that Satan liked it: fragile, broken, and dying. My body was fragile, my heart was broken, and a slow, painful death is what Satan had planned for me. Stress is a killer and worry causes you to be stressed.

Some of my most tiring days were when I tried to rest. There was no such thing as rest for my mind, yet when I worked so hard doing research that was stressing me also. I could not win no matter what I tried to do. But I had to do something because nothing else was working. I was still having my Bible studies and they were always encouraging, but that was the extent of my relaxation and encouragement.

When I got released from the hospital I went straight back home to my research and took up where I had left off. Nothing in my life had changed to release my stress level. Satan was chasing me all day long and everywhere I went, including church, he followed me there. I could not get away from him outside of my prayer closet.

There was always someone saying something that would cause me to doubt God's promises. The news-papers were relentless. It just seemed they would not give Jason a break of any kind. There seemingly was no way to escape Satan's power over my life. He used family, friends, newspapers, radios, and every other mechanism that he could to convince not only me, but my entire family, that Jason's life was headed for destruction.

Be sober, be vigilant, because your adversary the

devil, as a roaring lion, walketh about,

seeking whom he may devour

(1 Peter 5:8).

I became convinced from the very beginning that what happened to Jason was a vicious attack from Satan because Jason had just accepted God's call into the ministry six months before the tragedy. Satan was out to destroy Jason's faith and stop the work that Jason was doing for the Lord. However, I noticed

that Jason's faith remained constant. It never waiv-
ered. If only my faith could be as strong as my sons!

Ever since the tragedy, I look at each day through
different eyes, tear washed eyes. For it was only afterward that I could clearly see that every day the family
was together was a gift from God. Every birthday,
Easter, Mother's Day, Father's Day, Thanksgiving,
Christmas, and New Year's was a special gift from
God.

They were all treasures that for so long had been
taken for granted. Getting caught up in the hustle and
bustle of the holiday, how often did I stop and see
how fortunate and abundantly blessed I truly was?
It only takes one tragic event to get your attention.
When you see each day as possibly being your last it
brings entirely new meaning to life.

I can honestly say that I do try to live every day as if it were my last. What a wonderful world it would be if everyone lived their lives the same way. How sad it is that it took a tragedy of this magnitude in my own life to get my attention on what really matters in life!

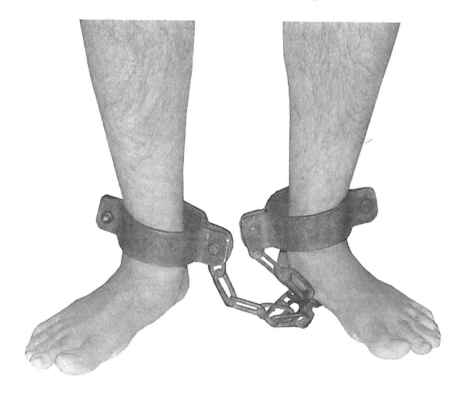

Chapter Ten

Toxic Cleansing

Long ago I had hung an imaginary sign on the door of my prayer closet that read: SATAN KEEP OUT! Remember, I had said earlier that the prayer closet was where I felt safe. It was my place of refuge where I felt protected and peaceful resting in God's Word. It was the place where I could find help for my weary mind. I decided that I was going to do the same thing with my body. I was hanging an imaginary sign over my head and over my heart saying: SATAN KEEP OUT! I totally rededicated my life, my body, my mind, and every ounce of my being to Christ. My being could no longer withstand the attacks from Satan that it was being hit with daily.

My confusion is continually before me, and the

shame of my face hath covered me

(Psalm 44:15).

I moved my mind and body into a different place. That new place was the book of Psalms, which had become a type of life support for my soul. I decided to hook myself up to it not only when I was having an anxiety attack but all of the time. It had become very apparent at that point that without God our family would be defeated by Satan and his minions. Nothing had gotten any better and it seemed to drastically get worse as the days went by. The case was lie built upon lie with no way to counteract any of it because we were under gag orders.

But what difference would it have made even if we could have spoken out? Then it would have become a "war of words" and the outcome would have been the same: a murder trial on April 13, 2009. I did not know whom I could trust and whom I could not trust anymore, but thank God there was a refuge, a hiding place where I could go to be with someone that I trusted with my own life as well as my son's life: God! I could not win the war that Satan was waging for my life in my own strength, but I could be victorious through the strength that God gave me.

Whom resist stedfast in the faith, knowing that the

same afflictions are accomplished in your brethren

that are in the world. But the God of all grace,

who hath called us unto his eternal glory by Christ

Jesus, after that ye have suffered a while, make you

perfect, stablish, strengthen, settle you

(1 Peter 5:9-10).

I felt like a new person in Christ. My heart had

a certain peace that it had not felt up to that point.

I felt as though all of the toxins and poisons had

been flushed out. I liked the new me. I was not only

reading my Bible in the evening, but I had it with me

all the time. I picked up inspirational books to get fur-

ther encouragement even if it was from people I had

never met, including people who knew absolutely

nothing about our situation but had experienced their own tragedies, and I had picked up the book *God's Shield of Protection: Psalm 91.*

I started fiercely claiming our miracle. I wiped away all doubt. Often when doubt tried to return I picked up my Bible to counteract Satan's attacks. I filled my days listening to praise songs as I worked. I did the same thing in my car. I never allowed myself to sit idle. I stayed busy sharing with my family passages from Psalm 91, always sending them something inspirational and showing them in God's Word what He says is ours in Christ.

My heart is fixed, O God, my heart is fixed: I will sing and give praise (Psalm 57:7).

Every time I heard a negative comment I used God's Word to counteract it. There was definitely a war being waged, but now I was on the winning side. PRAISE GOD!

In God I will praise his word, in God I have put

my trust; I will not fear what flesh can do unto me.

When I cry unto thee then shall mine enemies turn

back; this I know, for God is for me.

(Psalm 56:4-9).

At the name of Jesus, Satan has to flee. So much power is in the name of Jesus. My faith was the strongest it had ever been in my life. I had always heard it preached that faith was not built on the mountaintops, but it was built way down in the valley of the shadow of death. Now I knew exactly what that meant. Down in the valley I learned a lot of life lessons. I learned not to take one day for granted. I learned how easily life could be turned upside down and I learned how to obtain faith that would turn it right-side up! Most importantly, I learned what a weak useless person that I was in the flesh. There is no good thing in the fleshly mind.

But thank God I also learned from studying my Bible that this weak useless body can do all things through Christ who strengthens it. Christ can work inside of my body and mind if I will empty myself out and allow Him the room to do so. God has put a shield around my being. It's in front of me when one of Satan's darts comes at me. It is in back of me when Satan tries to sneak up on me from behind and it encompasses me when Satan tries to get his foot

through any opening. It only takes a small opening

for Satan to sneak in and destroy your entire life. In

my helpless state God knew my heart. He knew I

needed Him in order to survive and God did not turn

His back on me. Instead, God shielded me!

Wherefore take unto you the whole armour of God

that ye may be able to withstand in the evil day, and

having done all, to stand. Stand therefore, having

your loins girt about with truth, and having on the

breastplate of righteousness; And your feet shod

with the preparation of the gospel of peace. Above

all, taking the shield of faith, where with ye shall

be able to quench all the fiery darts of the wicked.

And take the helmet of salvation, and the sword

of the spirit, which is the word of God. Praying always with all prayer and supplication in the Spirit, and watching thereunto with all perseverance and supplication for all saints. And for me, that utterance may be given to me, that I may open my mouth boldly, to make known the mystery of the gospel, For which I am an ambassador in bonds: that therein I may speak boldly, as I ought to speak (Ephesians 6:13-20).

Oh, how I wished my entire family saw the world through my new tear-washed, spirit-filled eyes. I wanted each one of them to rise above their own doubts that Satan was flooding their lives with daily, but I could only build my own faith. However, I could and I did pray that God would also shield my family from the enemy and the darkness that he brings until they had their own strength to receive it for themselves. I could not wipe away their fear and doubts, but I could copy them continuously on Psalm 91 and God's promises. Everyone has to build their own faith on their own level with Christ. Building my faith to that high point was the hardest thing I had ever done in my entire life. Nothing about it had come without paying a dear price, but pain and suffering builds faith.

Chapter Eleven

A Way Out

I felt better than I had felt in a long time. It was two weeks before trial on a Sunday afternoon at 3:40 p.m. in a small country church where my son was the pastor. As Jim preached from the book of Psalms my mind veered off into a different direction. I had exhausted all of my earthly resources trying to help Jason, my research had come to an end, and I still had no more answers than I did before I started 10 months earlier as far as being able to show the judge something to totally exonerate Jason. To my knowledge no one had that missing piece that would help my son. The only thing that I succeeded in doing was wearing my physical body completely out.

I had no answers other than what God told me in His Word. However, I had learned a new lesson and that was to let God's Word be enough for me to believe and stop trying to do it myself. That was the hardest part to deal with. As a mother, how was I supposed to just give up on finding an answer? The answer is this: I already had found the answer and His name is Jesus. I could have saved my physical and mental being a lot of unnecessary pain and woe by totally trusting from the very beginning!

Hear my cry, O God, attend unto my prayer. From the end of the earth will I cry unto thee, when my heart is overwhelmed: lead me to the rock that is

higher than I. For thou hast been a shelter for me,

and a strong tower from the enemy, I will abide in

thy tabernacle for ever: I will trust in the

cover of thy wings (Psalm 61:1-4).

It was at that point that I came to the end of myself. I prayed silently at church: "God, I am so tired. I cannot do anything else for my son. I have done everything that I know to do. As much as I love Jason, You are his heavenly Father and You love him even more, so here he is! I am giving my son to You. I cannot fix it, but you can fix everything. I will not let Satan try to persuade me otherwise. I am stepping back from the entire situation. No more interference from me. I know that You have a master plan for Jason's life and I know that it is not to destroy him or his family. Thank you, Jesus, for relieving me from this awesome responsibility. I love you, Lord, and I know that You are going to take excellent care of 'our' son." In my mind's eye I could see me holding Jason in my arms. He was so heavy I felt as if I were about to drop him. But I handed Jason over to Jesus.

That was the second turning point in my life. The first was when I rededicated my body and mind to God and He healed me. I was turning Jason over to Him and it was at that time and place that a peace started moving from the bottom of my feet to the top of my head as Jesus was taking Jason out of my hands, lifting the burden off of my entire body, and taking my son into His care. How awesome that experience was! He knew my heart, He knew that I was sincere, and He knew that I was really walking away from it

and letting Him takeover. That was the moment that

I came to the end of myself and He gladly took it all

upon Himself. I could hear Him whisper, "It will all be

okay!" I could not stop crying, praising, and thanking

Jesus, for He is the way out of Satan's torment!

Humble yourselves therefore under the Mighty hand

of God, that he may exalt you in due time. Casting

all your care upon him, for he careth for you

(1 Peter 5:6-7).

I asked the Lord why it had to be so hard to get to

the end of myself and I heard Jesus say, "It's not hard

Jackie, you are the one that made it hard. I was right

there all the time but you just wouldn't give Jason to

Me even though you knew in your heart that I was more than capable of taking care of him. Always remember this Jackie: *"Trust in the unseen and not the seen! It is not hard, if you only believe."*

For we walk by faith and not by sight

(2 Corinthians 5:7).

Chapter Twelve

Satan's Snares

Isn't it so sad that after a wonderful spiritual experience with the Lord that Satan is right there the next day to try to steal it from you? It is like hearing Satan say, "Welcome back to the real world." He uses people and their tools such as telephones, computers, and other means of communication to bring you back down from the high place that you finally found in the midst of trials.

Satan does not want you on the mountaintop. He will use every means within his power to cast you back down into the lowest valley and destroy all hope that God has placed in your heart. Satan wanted nothing more than to destroy the wonderful hope and peace that I found in my Lord, Jesus Christ.

God already knew what the verdict in Jason's trial would be. I can't help but wonder if Satan knew at that point in time as well. I started to think that maybe Satan did already know what the verdict would be and he also knew that if he didn't destroy me first, come April 13, 2009 he would lose any power he had to destroy my life and that was why he was stalking my every move.

God is our refuge from the snares of Satan and He is sufficient. What is a snare? It is a trap. God doesn't have any desire to trap us. Why would He? God represents everything good. He is the Truth.

God is on our side and He is there to lift us up. It is always Satan who is there to bring us down. So many people blame God instead of blaming Satan for their depressed state of mind. Why would God want His people depressed, not wanting to face the day? Why would God want His people to have nightmares and live in constant fear? God says, "Fear not for I am with you always."

So what does Satan have to gain by placing snares into our life? There is a war being waged. It is a war between God and the evil one. Who wins this war? If you read the last chapter of the Bible you will see whom the winner really is.

And the devil that deceived them was cast into the lake of fire and brimstone, where the beast and the false prophet are, and shall be tormented

day and night for ever and ever

(Revelation 20:10).

Satan already knows who the winner is, for he has his appointed place in hell. So why is Satan concerned about my life and my family's life? Why has he taken time out of his busy schedule to try to destroy me? Could it be that when I am in a depressed state of mind that I am of limited use to God? I am not being a good witness for the Lord if I am living a defeated life. The less people that know about the Lord, the more people Satan will win to an eternal hell. That is what it is all about: heaven or hell. That is the bottom line.

What good is a depressed Christian for the army of the Lord? Depressed Christians do not even want to get out of the bed and face the day, let alone be an encouragement to the lost without Christ. It is not God's plan for His people to suffer affliction from Satan. It is our choice. How do we keep from living our lives in a depressed state of mind no matter what nightmares or snares that Satan throws our way to bring us down?

I found the answer to this most crucial question in my own life. I found it through heartache, tears, and total weariness in my own life. The answer is this: We have to stand strong in the victory that is already ours through Jesus Christ and walk in that power. We are in the army of the Lord and He has already defeated the enemy for us. Snares are on every side and we are on the frontlines of battle (spiritual warfare) every day that we live but we are here to occupy the land until He returns.

And having spoiled principalities and powers, he made a shew of them openly, triumphing over them in it (Colossians 2:15).

The only way that I found in my own life to overcome the enemy is to start my day in prayer. And it doesn't end there. Instead of listening to music that does not glorify God, I listen to praise songs. I talk with God continuously throughout the day. I started noticing how many times throughout the day that God intervenes on my behalf and I constantly thank Him.

We are not in this world by accident. We are here for a divine purpose. We who are born again

Christians are ambassadors for Christ. God needs each of us to share the gospel with others and even more as we see the day of his coming approaching.

Without God sending His angels to protect my life, I would never make it through the day without suffering harm. But as a child of God I rest on His promises that He keeps not only me, but my family also, underneath the shadow of His wings.

And the God of peace shall bruise Satan under your feet shortly. The grace of your Lord Jesus Christ be with you (Romans 16:20).

Chapter Thirteen

You May Come to Court, But Your Bible Can't

J ason and Steph listened to the attorney, taking in every piece of advice that was being given, wanting to make sure that they were fully under-standing everything. How hard it must have been for them to come by my house after that one last meeting at the attorney's office to give me more bad news. However, I had never come to expect any good news after those meetings. There was no such thing as a good meeting. It was always bad news and the latest meeting was no exception.

"We just left the attorney's office," Jason said, "and they went over some things with us concerning court on Monday. They wanted us to tell you that you should not bring your Bible to the courtroom because they feel that if any of the jurors are non-believers and they see you with a Bible, they could hold that against me."

I knew this was just another one of Satan's snares! See how Satan operates? I had turned everything over to the Lord and felt at peace so Satan had come to deliver another blow and what a whopping blow it was. I thought to myself, *What if I take my Bible to court and a juror finds it offensive and holds it against Jason and he goes to prison for 30 years just because I chose to bring my Bible to the courtroom?*

It would all be my fault for not taking the attorneys' advice. My action could very well be enough for the jury to deliver a guilty verdict. On the other hand, what if I did not take my Bible to court and I offended God? It came down to whom I was going to offend, a juror or God?

In God will I praise his word: in the Lord will I praise his word. In God have I put my trust: I will not be afraid of what man can do unto me. Thy vows are upon me, O God: I will render praises unto thee. For thou has delivered my soul from death: wilt not thou

deliver my feet from falling, that I may walk before

God in the light of the living? (Psalm 56:10-13).

I weighed the matter over and over in my mind. What if I took my Bible into the courtroom and a juror found it offensive enough to sentence my son to 30 years in prison over my action? But if I offend God and do not take my Bible with me and God does not deliver our miracle I will carry that guilt on my shoulders forever. Once again I had allowed Satan to place the burden back on my heart and life that I had given over to Jesus and He had so willingly relieved me of. It was more than I could carry on my shoulders so I took the whole matter into my prayer closet with me.

And I prayed, "Dear Lord, You know what I am up against here. If I cannot carry my Bible into the courtroom I have doubts that I will be able to physically endure the trial. Should I go to court? How can I not go? I have to be there for Jason. I have to know what my son's future holds. You are our only hope. You plainly tell us in Your Word that if we are ashamed of You before men, that You will be ashamed of us before our heavenly Father. I believe that I would rather offend a juror than offend You, Lord. I am putting this situation like all of the other horrific situations in Your hands. If You have promised me that You will take care of Jason, surely You will take care of this detail."

I took my Bible to court and it was the only thing that sustained me throughout the trial. Looking back on the matter now I fully believe it is where God tested my faith. It was Satan's one last attempt to persuade me to choose man over God. Was my relationship with God real or was I playing a game with God? That is where God gave me the opportunity to stand up for Him.

He already knew He would be standing up for our family, and most especially intervening on Jason's behalf. That was the place that I had to decide once and for all whether or not I trusted God. Had I made the decision not to take my Bible to court I believe God may not have shown up in the courtroom either. Thank God I did not let Satan sway me into leaving my Bible at home.

For this God is our God for ever and ever: he will be our guide even unto death (Psalm 48:14).

I now know that I put that additional pressure upon myself. There should never have been any doubt in my mind as to whether or not to take my Bible to court. I either trust God in all things or I do not trust God at all. There is no room for doubt! Doubt is due to the unnecessary fear factor.

Chapter Fourteen

He Was There All the Time

As Easter Sunday, April 12, 2009, was the day before trial, it was the saddest Easter we had ever spent together as a family. The newspaper headline read: "Veitch Murder Trial Begins Tomorrow." I did not even want to go to bed that night for I knew that as soon as I awoke I would have to face the *dreadful* day.

Monday, April 13, 2009, was the day my worst fear became reality. As I awoke my very first thought was, *Oh Lord, I cannot do this. There is no way that*

I can get out of this bed and face this day! It was then that I heard a small voice whisper, "How can you not? What would it do to Jason if he looked around and never saw your face in the courtroom? You may be that one ounce of strength that he is depending on just to survive this very day. Are you going to be that selfish and deny him that little bit of strength and encouragement that he is in desperate need of?" To which I replied, "Oh Lord, no! I am going to fight for my son to the very end. My son is innocent!"

With an angrier determination than ever I forced myself to get out of bed, get dressed, and go with Larry to the courthouse. I was angry because my son had been falsely accused of a crime that he did not commit, and angry because a prosecutor was determined to make some kind of example out of my son for defending his property, and angry because it had gotten that far and the false charges had not been dropped. I knew that somewhere in the midst of all the confusion there just had to be something good.

For four days our restless hearts had been forced to endure the torment to find the truth. For 10 long months it had been nothing but misery. I remember my sister Susie telling me 10 months ago that Jason may indeed have to endure a trial in order to defend his own innocence and to clear his own name. I never could bring myself to believe it would go that far. I always believed that the truth would come out somewhere along the way. I guess maybe it had in little pieces, but never in a way that led to a phone call saying that all the charges had been dropped.

I guess it took all the little pieces of truth along the way to come together in those four days in court for a jury of 12 to be able to form a full picture of what actually had happened. The puzzle was being put together piece by piece right there in that very court-room. The judge reminded the jury that anything they had heard, read in the newspaper, or saw on the tele-vision would not be allowed to play any part in their verdict. The only truth would be what was presented to them during the course of the trial. The truth had been unveiled. It was not pleasant. Nothing about the trial was pleasant. It hurt and I just wanted it all to go away. But God sustained me through those four days.

How did God sustain me? It was through the power of His Word. I was constantly reading the book of

Psalms throughout the trial. God was communicating with me right there in the courtroom. He told me just what I needed and wanted to hear. God would tell me things that the attorneys could not tell me. He told me He would bring forth the truth. God told me that He would take care of my son. He told me that no harm would beset us. In such a moment is there anything more encouraging that someone else could say to you?

Others could not take my pain away because they did not know what the outcome was going to be. Everything I was told from others was nothing more than false encouragement. The only One who gave me true encouragement was God. God was the only One that could untangle the mess. God was the only One that could make the mountain of lies built against my son fall like dominos. We were reminded that a case built on lies must crumble in court but the truth must stand!

Finally, it was time for jury deliberation. Closing statements by the attorneys had been made. The judge had charged the jury and sent them away to come back with a verdict that would either send my son to prison or send him home to his family. The moment of truth was at hand. There was nothing left to say to anyone. I wanted to seclude myself from the rest of the world.

I didn't want to hear what anyone else had to say because it didn't matter. Words from others did not help me. Only God's Word helped me. So I found a place on the front row of the courtroom, next to the wall and away from all the people. I did not want to leave the courtroom in case the verdict came, but I also did not want to sit around in the courtroom and chit-chat.

The jury had been in deliberation since the day before at 4:00 p.m. The judge sent us home at 6:00 p.m. and told us to return the next morning at 9:00 a.m. What a weary day it had been. It was approaching 1:00 p.m. and I could not sit there anymore. I gathered the family together and we formed a prayer circle outside the courtroom. Resisting all pride I converted one of the benches into an altar, where we prayed fervently with heavy, humble, and broken hearts for Jason's release. The people with joined hands in our prayer circle were the ones who wanted to witness the miracle that God had promised. The strength of the Lord that ran from hand to hand was what gave each of us what we needed just to go back into the courtroom.

Afterward, I returned to that same hard bench on the front row in the corner and back to the Psalms I went. It was at 3:30 p.m. that word came the jury had reached a verdict. There are no words to describe what was going on inside my mind and my heart. People were rushing around and hurriedly filling the courtroom. The attorneys busily instructed the family as to where we all should sit. Television cameras lined the back wall of the courtroom.

I did not want to leave my spot next to the wall in the corner on the front row. That had become my comfort zone, if there was such a thing. The whole situation was uncomfortable and it was not a place that I wanted to be. But that little spot in the corner was a type of prayer closet for me. I was away from the crowd and always comforted from God's Word. But just like so many other times over the course of the past 10 months that too was taken away from me during my time of greatest need. By that time there was standing room only in the courtroom.

I remember watching the jury come in and be seated. I remember the judge instructing the courtroom on what behavior would be accepted and what behavior would not be accepted after the verdict was read. It was so much like the "daymare" that I had. Was Jason about to be taken away from us? Was that nightmare on the verge of actually happening? I could hardly separate the bad dream from reality at that point.

I remember the foreman delivering a piece of paper to the judge with the verdict written on it. Isn't it amazing that such a small piece of paper carried such a large decision, one that would affect the rest of our lives? Since that moment in time I have so often thought about how big that tiny piece of paper was. How would that little piece of paper affect us? It could take away our son, it could take away my parents' grandson, it could take away Jim's brother, but most importantly, it could take away Steph's husband and J.J.'s daddy.

I remember squeezing my Bible. If I didn't have my Bible then what would I be holding onto? Larry is the love of my life, but Larry feared Jason would be sentenced to prison. What would have sustained me through those tormenting days in court? The judge looked at the piece of paper. Larry squeezed my hand. The judge asked Jason to stand up.

I thought to myself, *Oh God, it is so much like that nightmare I had earlier! Please don't let them take Jason away from his family. Oh God, please help us.* I could not breathe so I put my head down on my lap and Larry laid down on top of me, and that is when I heard the judge say, "We the jury find the defendant...*NOT GUILTY! NOT GUILTY OF ALL FIVE CHARGES!*"

Praise the Lord! I cried uncontrollably and for the first 10 minutes the only words that would come forth out of my mouth were: Thank You, Jesus! Thank You, Jesus! Thank You, Jesus! Larry was crying uncontrollably and everyone else was crying just like in my dream. But it was not sad crying, it was happy crying and praising, even the attorneys.

He shall send from heaven, and save me from the reproach of him that would swallow me up. Selah. God shall send forth his mercy and his truth (Psalm 57:3).

He shall call upon me, and I will answer him: I will be with him in trouble; I will deliver him, and honour him. With long life will I satisfy him, and shew him my salvation (Psalm 91:15-16).

God had kept His promise. The Lord did indeed take excellent care of "our" son Jason just like He promised me that He would. I wonder if that is the way it will be when we stand before the judgment seat of Christ? Family will not be with us. Attorneys will not be there to plead our case. God will pass down His verdict: heaven or hell. We must stand before God alone, and only believing in Christ saves us.

For we shall all stand before the judgment seat of Christ. For it is written, As I live saith the Lord, every knee shall bow to me, and every tongue shall confess to God. So then every one of us shall give account of himself to God (Romans 14:10-12).

The Times-Herald

CAMPUS

Monday,

Builder's murder trial Monday

Veitch trial Monday

Chapter Fifteen

Dawning of a New Day

After completing my first book *The Bridge: Between Cell Block A and a Miracle Is Psalm 91*, God gave me a revelation that touched my heart and let me know that I was now finished writing and the book had His stamp of approval. God pointed out to me that there were 15 chapters in the book, it was the 15th day of the month, and it had been 15 months since the tragedy. As I was telling my daughter-in-law Jennifer about that she said that the number 15 means REST! Unbeknownst to me at that time in another 15 months God would give me another revelation at the closing of this book. So I now know that the writing of this book also was totally under His inspiration and has His stamp of approval.

This is what God revealed to me about this book: As I was going for my morning walk and sipping on my coffee, stopping along the way to smell the roses and admiring God's beauty in watching the sun come up behind the trees, I started thanking God for letting our family experience the joy that comes in the morning after enduring all the weeping through all of those long nights for 10 months.

Out of nowhere God spoke up and said, "Jackie, you keep referring to the fact that you suffered for 10 long months. Let us figure out exactly how long the suffering lasted." When I calculated it down to the days it came out to be 9 months and 18 days from the time of the tragedy until the time of the verdict. God said to write that down and so I did. It looked like this: 9 18. God said to look at it like this:

Only with thine eyes shall thou behold and see the reward of the wicked (Psalm 91:8).

For all those long months Psalm 91 had been my life support and saving grace. God's shield of protection was the rock on which we had claimed and received our miracle and now God was still using Psalm 91 to give our book His stamp of approval.

Coweta track championships
held at Drake Stadium
— see results on page 6

POLLEN
COUNT

286
Extremely high
POLLENS PRESENT: Oak, sweetgum
and sycamore
Thursday's count for metro Atlanta

Confederate
Memorial Day
Saturday
— see page 3

The Times-Herald

1 Section, 12 Pages   145th year — Issue 107   Established 1866   Newnan, Georgia   ISSN NO. 0883-3536   50 cent

Friday, April 17, 2009

Coweta's Local Daily

Veitch cleared of all charges

By ALEX McRAE
alex@newnan.com

A Coweta County Superior
Court jury found Newnan builder
Jason Veitch not guilty of felony
murder and four other charges in
the June 28, 2008, shooting death
of Robert Mitchell, a drywall
worker who was shot to death by
Veitch at a home the defendant
was building in south Coweta.
Following the verdict Thursday

afternoon, friends, family and co-
workers of Veitch sat in
stunned silence while a host of
Veitch's family members and
friends sobbed audibly and
uttered cries of joy and relief.
Newnan attorneys Mike Kam
and Ron Harwell represented
Veitch. After the verdict, Harwell
said, "We grieve for the Mitchell
family and are thankful the jury
gave justice to Jason. This was a
just verdict. We are thankful for

the judicial system that provided a
free and fair hearing. Our justice
system is what separates us from
all other countries, and we appreciate the hard work of Mike Kam
and his staff for making sure the
truth came out at this hearing."
Veitch was acquitted on one
count of felony murder, three
counts of aggravated assault and
one count of possession of a
firearm while in the commission
of a felony.

Coweta Superior Court Judge
Dennis Blackmon presided over
the case. Coweta Judicial Circuit
Assistant District Attorney Ray
Mayer led the prosecution. Mayer
declined to comment immediately
after the verdict. Veitch also
declined to speak.

Conclusion

One of the experiences I had during the course of the trial was that I found myself asking the following questions over and over and over:

What if...the deceased had cooperated until the police arrived?

What if...law enforcement had not gotten lost in route?

What if...Jason had not gone to protect his houses?

What if...a deputy had not given Jason bad advice?

What if...I had accompanied Jason that night?

What if...the shotgun had not misfired?

What if...I had not believed Psalm 91?

What if...I had not taken my Bible?

For 10 months I wrestled with the "what if" factor. What if God doesn't help us? What if God lets Jason go to prison even though he is innocent? It was all of those "what if" questions that weakened my faith. It was only when I stopped questioning God and started trusting God that I obtained peace!

Why is it that so many people enjoy seeing bad things happen to good people? Why does bad news travel so fast? Why was it that all of those television cameras were so eager to follow the prosecutor and those with him to get their comments and stories? Why did they so easily disregard the revival going on inside the courtroom? Why is it that bad news gets all of the media attention? Why are so many people

discontent with their own lives? Why do people write

horrifying blogs about something without knowing

any of the details and why do so many of the people

reading those blogs choose to believe them? Who is

the master of deception? Who is the evil one? The

enemy of God and man is Satan and God warns us

over and over about our adversary and how to over-

come him.

In thee, O Lord, do I put my trust: let me never be

put to confusion (Psalm 71:1).

God has a valuable gift that He would like to offer

you. This gift may one day save your life. You may

think that you do not need this gift, but listen very

closely dear friend. Today your life may be just fine because you have absolutely nothing weighing heavy on your mind. You might not have anything keeping you awake at night. Make sure you thank God for that great blessing for that is exactly what my experience was a little over one year ago. But guess what? One call and that's all...everything radically changed in my life and not for the better. That is when you will come to appreciate this gift.

But remember it never hurts anything to be prepared before the unthinkable becomes a reality in your life. What happened in our family could very well happen in your family. Maybe not in the exact same way but it may be a tragedy nonetheless. Tragedy is no respecter of persons nor time and it can come in many different forms. It came to me like a thief in the night. It could come by way of a fatal health diagnosis or an unexpected death in the family. There are so many different avenues tragedy can come through and attack us. I fully believe that if you live long enough you will experience tragedy at least once in your lifetime. No one is immune!

As far as tragedy not being a respecter of time let me give you another example of tragedy striking in our family in the early morning hours that could just have easily happened in your family and possibly already has happened. I was not aware of Psalm 91 at the time; however, I do pray for protection over my family every morning and I fully believe that praying for protection that Friday morning did come in to play as my oldest son Jim left his house around 9:00 a.m.

As he was headed toward town a car completely out of control came around the curve at a high rate of speed and behind the wheel was a drunk driver who had been partying all night and was driving home in the morning. The driver of that out-of-control car crossed the center line and hit my son head-on. That tragedy could have taken away my son's life at that very moment. No one could believe that he had escaped without fatal injuries. But God intervened on Jim's behalf. Jim is a pastor and Satan tried very hard that morning to take away Jim's life, but God had a plan for my son. That plan was to continue preaching the gospel of Christ.

Satan had a plan on April 16, 2009 to take away my youngest son's life, but God had another plan for Jason's life. That plan was to continue preaching the gospel of Christ. Now here is the gift that I would like to offer you today: JESUS! Invite Christ into your life by making Him your personal Lord and walk in light of your liberation from the snares of Satan! If you have already invited Christ into your life please claim Psalm 91 over your life as well as your loved ones everyday. It is an added benefit that God grants His children. If and when tragedy does come your way, before turning to the world for help, run to God for He alone has every answer that you stand in need of.

Be thou my strong habitation, whereunto I may continually resort: thou hast given commandment to save me, for thou art my rock and my fortress (Psalm 71:3).

CPSIA information can be obtained at www.ICGtesting.com
Printed in the USA
LVOW060748020212

266635LV00001B/1/P